Tawny

Snoopy

THIRSTY SLURP

Dov

Our

D0938593

Irene
and
Greybird

Scrappy

Bebe

Brody

For my older sister, Pam, who was my babysitter.
And for my nieces, Kathy, Karen, Kris,
and Josi, whom I watched over.
We made each other crazy. I laugh about it still.

And a special thank-you to Caleb and Corina, who gave this book its title.

Sitting Duck
Copyright © 2010 by Jackie Urbanovic

Manufactured in China.
All rights reserved. No part of this book may be used or reproduced in any manner
whatsoever without written permission except in the case of brief quotations embodied in
critical articles and reviews. For information address HarperCollins Children's Books, a
division of HarperCollins Publishers, 10 East 53rd Street, New York, NY 10022.
www.harpercollinschildrens.com

Library of Congress Cataloging-in-Publication Data is available.
ISBN 978-0-06-176583-4 (trade bdg.) — ISBN 978-0-06-176584-1 (lib. bdg.)

Typography by Rachel Zegar
10 11 12 13 14 LEO 10 9 8 7 6 5 4 3 2 1
❖
First Edition

SiTTiNG DUCK

Jackie Urbanovic

HARPER
An Imprint of HarperCollins Publishers

"Babysitting is easy!" said Brody. "When Anabel gets here, we'll all play together. Our only job will be to keep her out of trouble."

"Sure," said Max. "How much trouble could a puppy get into, anyway?"

"Babysitting, huh?" said Chloe. "It sounds like a LOT of trouble to me."

"I suggest we make a run for it. Everyone else is going," said Dakota.

"UNCLE BRODY!"
said Anabel.

"Anabel, this is your Uncle Max and Uncle Dov," said Brody.

SMACK!

HIYA! HIYA!

"LET'S PLAY!" shouted Anabel.

They played dress up . . .

and silly faces . . .

and chef . . .

and ball. . . .

Brody sat Anabel down for a story and a nap.
"Does this mean we aren't going to play hide 'n'
seek?" asked Anabel.

"Just listen and—yawn—relax," said Brody.
So Anabel listened and Brody, well, relaxed.

UNCLE MAXIE!

"I thought you were napping!" said Max.

"Uncle Brody's napping. I want to go outside!" said Anabel.

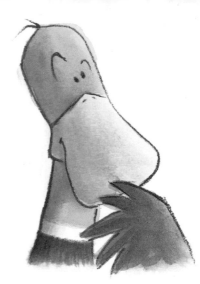

"Outside?" Max considered the idea.
"Well, I did want to get some outdoor
shots . . . and how much trouble could a
puppy get into, anyway?"

"YIPPPPEEEEEEEE!"

yelled Anabel.

"SHHHHHHHHH!"
said Max.

"What would you like to do?" asked Max. "Swing?"
"EEK!" said Anabel.

"Swim?" suggested Max.
"I don't think so . . ." said Anabel.

"Bounce?" asked Max.

"YES, BOUNCE!" said Anabel.

"Okay, then! Ready, set, GO!" said Max.

"CLICK"

They bounced!
They flew!

Up and down.
Higher and higher.

Until Max realized he was bouncing alone.

"Anabel?"

"Anabel?"

"ANABEL!

WHERE ARE YOU!?" shouted Max.

"UP HERE, UNCLE MAX!" Anabel called, giggling.

"DON'T MOVE, ANABEL!
NOT ONE INCH! I'M GOING
TO GET HELP!" yelled Max.

Max returned with Brody and an idea. "I'll pull down on the branch until you slide off," Max explained.

"Okay, Uncle Max," said Anabel.

"Be careful now," warned Brody.

"GRAB MY
LEGS, BRODY!"
yelled Max.
"PULL!"

"Oops!"

"UNCLE MAAX

cried Anabel.

"I'M COMING!" Max called,
while Brody pushed the trampoline
toward Anabel to cushion her fall.

"AIM FOR THE TRAMP!!" yelled Brody.
And she did. With a little help.

WHOOMP!

Anabel bounced to safety along with—*BOING*—
her—*BOING*—rescuers—*BOING, BOING!*

"Anabel," gasped Max. "Are you all right?"
"That was FUN, Uncle Max! Let's do it again!" said Anabel.

At six p.m. Irene returned home.

"Okay, I can take Anabel home now. Where is she?"

"Napping," said Moosay.

"So it went well?" asked Irene.

"FINE!" said Scrappy.

"No problem," said Chloe.

"Really," said Tawny. "How much trouble could a puppy get into, anyway?"